3

A GILBERT MORRIS MYSTERY

MOODY PRESS
CHICAGO

©2000 by
GILBERT MORRIS

ISBN: 0-8024-4027-4

1 3 5 7 9 10 8 6 4 2

Printed in the United States of America

Contents

Too Smart Jones in Charge

Juliet Too Smart Jones lay on her bed. Her eyes were half closed. She'd been staring thoughtfully at the pictures on her wall.

Juliet's room was neat, but it was packed with all the things that ten-year-old girls like to collect. There were posters. There were pictures of friends on every wall. Her light blue chest of drawers held more pictures of friends and fun times.

She smiled at a big photo that had been on the wall only a short time. It was a picture of Juliet herself. She was holding up a diamond necklace. Her friends Mr. and Mrs. Del Rio were on each side of her. Their arms were around their grandchildren, Samuel and Delores.

Juliet remembered how she had solved the case of the buried treasure. All the home-schooled boys and girls in Oakwood had tried to find out who owned those buried jewels. Juliet smiled again as she thought, *But I was the one who solved the mystery.*

She sighed happily and got up from her bed. She was wearing a pair of Gap jeans and her favorite lime green shirt. Her older brother, Joe, had said, "You don't even take that shirt off to wash it." It was true that lime green was her favorite color. But she had told Joe that she had *three* lime green shirts. She didn't always have on the same one.

She stopped in front of the mirror to see if she had changed any since the last time she had looked at herself. She leaned closer and studied her face. She saw auburn hair with a natural curl and large brown eyes. She had to wear glasses for reading. They were big black-rimmed ones that made her feel very grown-up.

Suddenly the door burst open, and her brother came shooting in like a cannonball. "Hey!" he shouted. "What are you—"

"Don't bother to knock, Joe!" Juliet said, turning to meet him. "Just come busting right in anytime you want!" Her brother had red hair and blue eyes exactly like their dad's. Juliet loved Joe dearly, but sometimes he could be very pesky.

"Well, excuse me! I didn't know you were the queen of England!" he said. He was wearing a pair of ragged cutoffs and a worn T-shirt that had a picture of a tiger on the front. He put his hands on his hips. "You don't knock when you come into *my* room."

"Yes, I do!"

"No, you don't!"

Juliet sniffed. "I'm not going to argue with you. What do you want?"

"Well, I was going to ask you to go exploring with me. But I don't know as you deserve a break as good as that!"

Juliet scowled at him. "What do you mean, 'break'?"

Joe grinned broadly. "Think of all the people that would like to go exploring in the woods with me."

"Name two."

"I could name a hundred. But if you don't want to go, I'll go by myself."

"Wait a minute!" Juliet really loved to go exploring with Joe. Besides, they were working on a leaf project. Joe was a year younger than she was, but he knew the names of lots of trees and bushes and flowers. And besides *that,* the sun was shining brightly, and Juliet was ready to get out of the house. "Maybe I will go with you. You might get lost."

"Get lost! I got a compass. Why would you say a thing like that?"

"I'd think you would remember the last time we went exploring. We got so lost that we thought we'd never get back!" *She* well remembered the time. They had gotten themselves completely turned around in the woods. That was when they had come upon Amos Redfield's house.

Joe paid no attention at all to what she'd said. He said, "Well, make up your mind. If you want to come with me, you'd better come on. I'm not going to wait forever."

"All right, all right. I'll go—but only if I get to be in charge."

"Do I hear Too Smart Jones talking again?"

Juliet had been tagged with the nickname Too Smart Jones for some time. She hated it. When she first came to Oakwood, she'd even pretended to be dumb—just so she wouldn't get that nickname in a new town. Her plan had not worked.

"Don't call me Too Smart!" she said in a loud voice. "I've told you that a hundred times! Anyway, I'll go along—just to be sure you don't get yourself lost."

Joe headed toward the stairs without her.

Juliet grabbed a heavy sweatshirt, pulled it over her head, then dashed out the door after him.

They ran downstairs, and Joe made straight for the kitchen. "Mom, we've got to have some food. We're going exploring. We want to hunt for new leaves for our project."

Mrs. Jones had hair the same color as Juliet's and the same warm brown eyes. She was peeling potatoes. She looked at them and turned her head to one side. She said, "Don't get lost."

Joe waved his arms. "Why does everybody tell me not to get lost? I never get lost."

Their mother smiled. "I just wanted to warn you to be careful."

"I feel insulted. Do I get the cookies or not, Mom? It looks like you ought to give me something after that."

Laughing, Mrs. Jones walked over to a cabinet. "I've got some all ready for you. Some, but not too many. I don't want you to spoil your supper."

"Thanks, Mom." Joe took the plastic-wrapped packages. He handed one to Juliet. Then he started for the hall closet. "Got to get my backpack and notebooks and stuff," he said.

"You keep an eye on Joe, now, Juliet. He tends to get overexcited. He might wind up in California."

Juliet went over and gave her mother a good-bye hug. "Don't worry. It'll be all right this time, because *I* get to be in charge."

Juliet and Joe went down the walk toward the picket fence that went all around their house. They turned onto Chestnut Drive, then onto Main Street. Juliet listened as Joe happily described an invention he was working on.

"It's going to make me rich and famous,"

11

he said. He always waved his hands around when he talked. Also he had the habit of sometimes grabbing his hair and pulling at it.

"It doesn't sound like it would work to me," she said, frowning.

"That's because you're not an inventor like I am," Joe said.

A yellow cat came out from behind a tree and looked at them. Joe called to him, and the cat turned and fled. Then he said, "This invention is going to be the greatest thing since buttons on a shirt."

"So tell me again what it does."

"Well," he said, "you know how, when you come into a room that's dark, you can't see where the light switch is?"

"Sure I know about that."

"My invention will be a lighted wall switch. Every switch in the house will glow. So all you have to do is reach out and turn it on."

"Well, that sounds more sensible than some of the things you've tried to invent. But I think somebody's already invented it."

"They haven't, either."

The two argued until they came to the ballpark. There they stopped long enough to watch Flash Gordon and Chili Williams, two other homeschoolers. They were playing catch.

"How's it going, Flash?" Joe called out.

Melvin "Flash" Gordon turned his wheelchair around and rolled toward them. He was ten. He had bright green eyes and hair almost the same color as Juliet's. "Hey, everything's copacetic."

Juliet laughed at him. "You don't know what that means!"

"Sure I do, but I bet Joe doesn't."

Joe, indeed, did not seem to know what the word meant. But he pretended not to care. He snorted. "You don't know, either! You just made it up!"

The other boy came over to join them. Chili Williams, age nine, grinned happily. His skin was as black as it could be. His large ears stuck out. Someone said he looked like a car with the doors left open. Chili got his nickname because he loved chili. He would even eat it for breakfast.

"What's going down?"

"We're going out to the woods and look for leaves for our project."

"Better stay and play handball," Chili said. "I'm going to beat the socks off Mr. Flash Gordon."

Juliet knew the two boys had worked out a new set of rules for handball. They could play handball even with Flash in his wheelchair.

"I'll tell you what," Joe said. "I'll come back and beat you both when I get through collecting some leaves."

"Take it easy."

Flash and Chili waved good-bye.

As Juliet and Joe walked along, Joe said thoughtfully, "Flash has a big problem—having to be in that wheelchair. But I don't know anybody that handles a problem better than he does."

"Every time I get to thinking *I've* got a problem," Juliet said, "I think about him. And then my problems don't look so big."

"He says God is going to make him well someday."

"Maybe He will. Wouldn't that be wonderful?"

Flash was the son of a preacher. Reverend Gordon had a very small church. He had to work in construction to earn the money they needed. Still, Flash's parents were cheerful people. And Flash himself was the most cheerful of all the homeschoolers.

Juliet and Joe walked all the way through town. On the other side of town was a large wooded area. It was filled with large trees, saplings, and brush. In some places, the trees and brush were so thick that it was impossible to get through. That's where they were headed.

When they passed the Del Rio house, Juliet saw Samuel and Delores. They were playing on the monkey bars. Juliet waved.

"They can do stuff on those bars that would break my neck," Joe said.

"Well, they were trained to be acrobats in the circus. Delores told me they started her doing acrobatics when she was only two years old."

They stood watching Delores and Samuel for a while. Then they invited the Del Rios to join them looking for leaves in the woods.

"Can't," Samuel said. He jumped straight up into the air and turned a standing back flip. It looked easy. Juliet knew she could never do that in a million years.

"We've got some family coming to our house," Samuel said then. "We've got to be here to meet them."

"Maybe we can go later, though. How long will you be in the woods?" Delores asked.

"If Joe doesn't get us lost, we'll be back in a couple of hours. If he does, you may never see us again."

Joe picked up a handful of dirt and rushed toward her. "I'll wash your face!" he cried.

Juliet took off running. "You leave me alone, Joe!"

The Del Rio children stood watching them go.

"I wish I was as smart as Juliet," Delores said wistfully.

Samuel put his arm around her. "We're not as smart as Too Smart Jones, but she can't do a backward somersault like we can."

2

Something Wicked
This Way Comes?

Hey, look over there! What's that?"

Juliet looked up from where she was picking a small flower for her collection. She squinted and said, "Well, it looks like a dog to me."

Juliet and Joe had been wandering all over the woods. It had been very quiet, and Juliet had not heard any barking. But there the scruffy brown dog was. He had just appeared out of nowhere. He was not a large dog, and his fur was long and ratty.

"That's a funny looking dog. What breed is he, anyway?"

"I think he's like Heinz ketchup," Joe said, laughing. "The Heinz ketchup people say they make sixty-seven different kinds of ketchup. Looks like that dog's got a little bit of everything in him—from a collie down to a poodle."

The brown dog looked at Juliet and Joe as if wondering if he should come up to them. Suddenly he barked—once, at first. Then he barked a series of little barks.

"What's he barking at?" Juliet asked.

"I don't know. Can't see that he's got a collar on. Come here, boy!" Joe whistled.

But the dog just stood very still.

"I've seen that dog somewhere before," Joe said. "But I can't remember where."

"Well, you won't be likely to see him again. There he goes."

They watched as the dog disappeared. And then Joe shrugged. "I guess he's just a stray from someplace."

Too Smart Jones had the habit of filing away all sorts of things in her mind. Sometimes she would simply look at a license plate and remember it—for no reason except that the car was pretty. She thought about that scruffy brown dog showing up out of nowhere. And she filed that away in her mind.

Then Juliet said, "Let's go look for some more leaves." She took a piece of bright pink paper from her backpack. She tore off a piece and stuck it onto the branch of a tree.

"I still think that's dumb!" Joe said as he watched. "We're not going to get lost."

"No, we're not. We're not because I'm leaving a trail." She looked back and could see two other pieces of pink paper that she had left.

"We can get right back where we came from by following these."

"Aw, you're too careful. Nothing's going to happen."

Juliet did not pay him any mind. She had learned long ago that there was no point in arguing with Joe Jones. She just kept on leaving bits of pink paper as they headed deeper into the woods.

The sky was clear, and the air was cool. Overhead, fleecy clouds were drifting gently across the blue sky. From time to time a bird would lift its voice in song. One time they were startled when a possum suddenly appeared. But then it scurried off.

After a while they came to a clearing and a small stream. Joe pointed and said, "Let's sit down here and eat some cookies. My feet need to get some rest."

"Sounds good to me."

Juliet and Joe sat down by the water and brought out the packages of cookies that their mother had given them.

Joe ate one. "Boy, these are the world's best cookies!"

"How would you know? You ate that one so fast you didn't have a chance to taste it!"

"That's what you think." Then he glanced over at Juliet's cookies. "Are you going to eat all of yours?"

"Yes, I am going to eat all of mine. You can't have any. You have your own!"

They argued for a while. But Juliet wound up giving Joe three of her cookies.

Then she suddenly straightened up and stared across the small clearing. "Did you see that, Joe?"

"Did I see what?"

"There. Right over there. I think I saw somebody."

Joe swallowed his last bite of cookie and looked where Juliet was pointing. He stared hard and then said, "I think I saw somebody, too."

"We'd better get out of here, Joe."

"No. You wait right here. I'm going to circle around and find out who it is—or what it is."

"It could just be that dog we saw . . ."

"No. He'd come right out if it was." Joe put a finger to his lips and motioned to Juliet to stay where she was. He got up quietly and left her.

Joe Jones was not very good at writing papers. He was not very good at writing anything. But he was very good at creeping through the woods. He had learned how to walk quietly and not step on any dead sticks. He made his way around a thick growth of trees to the other side of the clearing. And when Joe got there, he found what he was looking for.

It's Billy Rollins and Jack Tanner, he thought. He grinned, for he just then had a good idea. *Bet they were going to sneak up and scare Juliet and me. I think I'll just give them a little scare.*

Joe kept out of sight, but he managed to get just behind where the two boys were crouching. This was going to be fun. Billy Rollins needed to be scared. He was a bully and a show-off. Jack Tanner used to be Billy's good friend. And now he was back to spending a lot of time with Billy again. Both boys kept looking toward where Juliet still sat.

Joe sneaked up very carefully. Suddenly he leaped out at them, screaming with all his might. *"Yaaaaaaaa!"*

Billy Rollins and Jack Tanner both jumped straight up in the air. They began running through the brush.

"Hey, where you guys running to?" Joe called after them.

Billy and Jack stopped and looked back. When Billy saw Joe standing there and laughing at them, his face turned angry and red.

"What do you mean sneaking up and scaring somebody half to death?"

"Well, that's what you were going to do to Juliet and me."

"We were not!"

Juliet came up beside Joe, laughing. "I didn't know you could jump that high, Billy. You ought to go out for the high jump."

Jack seemed to think he had to act tough. He turned on Joe. "I ought to black your eye for doing that!"

Juliet said at once, "No, you were getting ready to scare *us*, so you got just what you deserved!"

Billy Rollins said, "Come on, Jack. We don't have time to fool with these two."

As the boys started to stomp away, Billy yelled back, "You two are going to get yours someday! You're not as smart as you think you are, Too Smart Jones!"

Juliet and Joe turned away, still laughing.

Juliet said, "You did fine, Joe."

"Well, it was fun all right, and they sure deserved to get scared."

They started back through the woods. But they had not gone very far when suddenly the scruffy brown dog appeared once more.

"There's that dog again, Joe. Is he following us?"

"I don't know. But I don't think so. He doesn't stay *with* us."

"Maybe he's hungry."

"Maybe so, but we ate all of the cookies. We don't have anything to feed him."

And then Joe looked at the sky. All its blue had turned to gray, and the wind was blowing through the tree branches. "Besides," he said, "it looks like rain. Maybe we'd better head for home."

"All right. There's the first pink paper." Juliet picked it off the thornbush she had put it on. As they came to the pink papers, she put each one of them in her pocket.

Very large trees grew in this part of the woods. Juliet began to think there was something scary about the dark spaces between the trees.

Once she stopped dead still. "Did you hear something, Joe?"

"Did I hear what?" he asked.

She turned around and stared into the dark woods behind them. "I thought I heard . . . something."

Joe looked for a long time. But then he shook his head. "I didn't hear anything. And I don't see anything."

"Well, come on. Let's hurry."

Juliet and Joe began to hurry. But a few minutes later she stopped again and turned around. "I *know* I heard something that time!"

"If you did, it was probably just Billy and Jack trying to scare us again."

By now Juliet was getting truly frightened. "Let's get out of here. Fast."

And they started to run.

"Slow down," Joe said, breathing hard. "You don't have to run *that* fast!"

He was probably scared himself, Juliet thought. But Joe Jones would never admit it.

They reached the edge of the woods, still at a run. Both were gasping for breath. Joe said, "See? We didn't get lost."

"That's because I marked the trail." And then Juliet grabbed his arm. "Look over there, Joe," she whispered. "Walking toward the trees."

Joe looked. "Yeah, I see him. It's an old man—and that brown dog's with him. Must be *his* dog. Do you know him?"

Juliet was thinking hard. "I saw him once before. It was in town one night, sort of late. I was walking home with Jenny—it was the night she was going to sleep over at our house. We saw him over on Elm Street. He was kind of shuffling along. He looked a little scary . . ."

"You think he's a robber or something? He looks too old to be a robber, Juliet."

"I didn't think of that at the time, but . . . he just looks so old and spooky."

They watched the old man shuffle along the edge of the woods. Then he disappeared among the trees. The small dog looked back. He gave one sharp bark, and then he disappeared, too.

"Well, they're gone," Joe said. "And *we'd* better get gone and get home."

Juliet Jones kept wondering about the old man all the way home. Sometimes she just couldn't put things out of her mind. She knew she would still be thinking about him after she went to bed. *It's another mystery,* she thought. *I'm going to do a little investigating about that old man, whoever he is.*

Joe glanced over at her. "I know what you're doing," he accused. "You're thinking about how you found another mystery."

Juliet said, "You don't know everything!"

"I know you, though." Joe grinned. "And you're thinking that you've got to have another mystery to solve. Well, that old man's probably just somebody who lives in the next town. That's why we haven't seen him much."

Juliet did not argue, but she was thinking, *Tomorrow I'll find out who he is. And maybe I can learn something about where he came from.*

3

Something to Pray For

Mealtime at the Jones household was always fun. Mrs. Jones was a good cook, and the family enjoyed being together.

They had a big round dining-room table. Mr. Jones had chosen it himself. He said, "There is no head or foot to this table, so we can all reach out and get what we want."

Juliet's father was a tall man with red hair and blue eyes. He worked at building bridges and skyscrapers. His hands were callused and strong. He was also what Joe called a "health nut." There were exercise machines inside the house, racing bicycles outside, and Mr. Jones was always jogging.

Tonight he had grilled the steaks for dinner. Juliet started the baked potatoes. Her mother made a delicious salad and had baked bread to go with the meal.

Halfway through eating, her father said, "Joe! Don't eat so fast. There's plenty of food here."

"He has no manners at all, Dad," Juliet said. She was cutting up her steak into small, bite-sized portions. "Look at him. He spilled lettuce all over the tablecloth."

"It'll wash," Joe said cheerfully. He had a ring of food around his plate—lettuce, bread crumbs, gravy stains, and fragments of his potato. "It's just sooooo good, Mom! I just can't help gobbling it down."

"I know what you're trying to do. You're trying to butter me up so that I'll give you a double helping of dessert." But his mother smiled.

"I didn't even know we were going to have dessert," Joe said innocently.

"Yes, you did too!" Juliet said. "We *always* have dessert. Mom's exactly right, and I don't think you ought to get any extra."

"I don't tell *you* how to eat!"

"Well, you need more manners," Juliet said primly. She knew she was being bossy. She really had been trying to do better, but being bossy just seemed to come naturally, especially with Joe.

"Let me tell you what happened in the woods today, Dad," Joe said eagerly.

"No! I want to tell," Juliet cried.

"I thought of it first. Now, you let me tell."

"Let him talk, but don't strangle yourself on that roll, Joe," their father warned.

"Well, we were out in the woods, and we saw this scruffy dog—"

"You forgot to tell how I marked the way so we could find our way back," Juliet interrupted.

"That's not important! We could have found our way back, anyway! Well, we saw this scruffy dog, and then we heard something. And we thought maybe it was somebody sinister out in the woods."

Joe liked to learn new words, and "sinister" was his word this week. Everything was "sinister"!

"So I left Juliet where she was, and I snuck around and—"

"There's no such word as 'snuck,'" Juliet told him.

"Sure there is," Joe said. "I sneak today, and yesterday I snuck."

"Go on, Joe. What happened?" Mr. Jones asked.

"Well, it was that old Billy Rollins and Jack Tanner. They were getting ready to scare us, and I scared the soup out of *them*. You should have seen them jump!"

Juliet nodded and laughed. "It *was* funny. They were going to scare us, and Joe scared them instead."

"But that's not what I want to tell you

about, Dad," Joe said quickly. "We were coming back, and it was getting stormy, and suddenly we thought somebody was after us. Then we saw this sinister looking old man creeping up on us."

"He was not creeping up on us! He was just walking beside the woods!" Juliet insisted.

"Well, he would have been creeping up on us if we wouldn't have seen him!"

"What old man was this?" their mother asked. "Did you know him?"

"I saw him once before." Juliet told how she had seen the old man with the dog in town. "I'm going to find out more about him, too."

"Aw, she's always looking for some mystery to solve. She thinks she's Sherlock Holmes."

"I do not!"

"Well, Sherlock was a pretty good detective," Mr. Jones said. "Maybe when you grow up you'll be a lady detective, Juliet. And you'll be a much prettier detective than Sherlock Holmes, I'm sure."

"I'd like that!" Juliet said quickly. "It would be fun to solve mysteries and get paid for it."

Juliet helped her mother with the dishes, and then the four of them got out the Monopoly board. Monopoly was one of Juliet's favorite games. Joe often won, though. Tonight he was unbeatable.

When Juliet lost again, he said, "Too Smart Jones bites the dust!"

"Don't call me that!"

"No, don't call her that, Joe," their mother said. "It isn't kind to use nicknames that people don't like."

Joe said, "I wouldn't care if they called *me* Too Smart. I wouldn't want anybody calling me Too-Dumb, though."

The evening passed, and finally Juliet went to bed. As she did every night, she knelt down beside her bed to pray. She prayed for her parents. She prayed for Joe. She prayed for the homeschool kids that she knew best. And for *their* parents. And then she began to pray that she would find out who the old man with the dog was.

"It seems a funny thing to pray about, Lord, but I'd like to know who he is. Maybe he needs help. So I'm asking You to help me find out something about him. And if You want me to help him, I'll do that too—if You'll show me how."

Juliet finished her prayer and jumped into bed. But before she closed her eyes, she looked out her window. A big yellow moon was high in the sky. She thought, *It was nice of God to make the moon. It's so pretty.*

She thought one more time about the old man and the scruffy dog. And then Too Smart Jones drifted off to sleep.

4

More
Mystery

Joe stood back and admired the poster that he had pinned to the wall. On it were samples of the different leaves that he and Juliet had found. Juliet had wanted to put them all in a row. But Joe was more artistic. He had placed them in pretty patterns.

"They look great, don't they?"

Juliet was flexing her fingers. She had been writing a short paragraph to glue under each leaf. "It does look good," she had to admit. "You always can fix things to look pretty."

"Well, I want our poster to be the best one. You think we have enough leaves?"

"I think so. Mom said that it was more important to have a pretty display—with good descriptions—than to have a lot of them."

"Well, that's good. And it sure was more

fun hunting leaves in the woods than doing some of the other stuff we've had to do."

Juliet and Joe continued to work on the poster until their mother appeared at the classroom door. "Come on, you two. It's time to eat lunch."

"Hooray! My stomach thinks my throat's been cut!" Joe exclaimed.

"I wish you wouldn't say those awful things!" Juliet said. "It's not nice."

Joe merely grinned at her. "You're just mad because you didn't think of it yourself."

Lunch was tuna sandwiches with dill pickles and potato chips. Joe wolfed his down hungrily and then said, "Mom, why can't we have a milkshake machine?"

"Because you don't need a lot of milkshakes."

"I can make a milkshake machine," Joe said thoughtfully. "It would be real easy."

"Oh, no! Not another invention!" Juliet groaned.

"Why not? Besides, you like milkshakes as good as I do. Give me a piece of paper, Mom. I'll draw out a picture of it."

"We don't have time for that," Juliet said. "We've got our chores to do."

"Aw, I want to go play ball!"

"You can do that after you do your chores," his mother promised.

Juliet and Joe finished eating. Then they

threw themselves into their chores at break-neck speed. Neither of them really minded doing jobs around the house, but Joe complained about it almost every day.

"You ought to read the stories in the book of Exodus," Juliet said as they vacuumed the living-room floor.

"I have."

"Don't you remember what happened when the people complained?"

Joe thought for a minute. "The earth opened up and swallowed them?"

"Yes. And the preacher said they ought to call Exodus the book of complaining. Over and over again the people would complain, and then God would have to punish them for it."

Joe turned off the vacuum cleaner and looked around at the clean room. "All right. I won't complain anymore. Well, the work's all done. I'm going and play ball with Chili and Flash. Maybe Samuel will be there."

"I'll meet you later."

"Where are you going?"

"Oh, I think I'll go see Jenny. And maybe Delores will be there, too. I hope we can go to Delores's house and play dress up again."

"That's no fun. You ought to play ball."

But Juliet merely shook her head. She put away the vacuum cleaner. Then she changed into a pair of light tan shorts. She tucked in a blue shirt, slipped into her Keds, and left the house.

She enjoyed the beautiful fall weather. It was cool, and Juliet always liked this time of year. Now it made her remember that Halloween was coming soon.

Most of the homeschoolers did not celebrate Halloween. Their parents thought that pretend witches were too close to real witches. Instead, the homeschool boys and girls had a big scavenger hunt. Juliet thought that was more fun than she had ever had on Halloween, anyway.

She walked on down to Court Street, looking at the old houses as she went. Most of them were old-fashioned but were freshly painted. Big oak trees towered over the street, too, making an avenue. And then she heard her name being called.

Juliet looked around. "Hi, Jenny," she said. "That's a new outfit you have on."

"Oh, no, I just haven't worn it in a long time." Jenny White was one year younger than Juliet. Her father had been killed in an accident, so her mother was her only parent.

"Where are you going?" Jenny asked.

"I was going to your house to see you. I thought maybe we could go over to Delores's and play dress up."

Jenny smiled sweetly. She was shy except around people she knew well, and she knew

Juliet very well. "That suits me fine! And guess what?"

"I give up."

"Mom is going to marry Mr. Tanner next month. Isn't that neat?"

"Oh, that's so wonderful, Jenny! Then you'll have both a mom and a dad."

But suddenly Jenny sighed. "Sometimes I don't know. It'll be . . . different."

Jenny looked so strange that Juliet asked, "What's the matter?"

"Well, I'm all of a sudden going to have a new brother too. And I don't know if I like that part."

Mr. Tanner had one boy, Jack. He was ten years old.

"Why, it'll be OK. You see how much fun Joe and I have together," Juliet said.

"But that's different. You grew up together. Here, I didn't have any brothers, and now all of a sudden I'll have one. He's been pretty mean to me sometimes, too—at least when Billy Rollins is around. Jack always does everything Billy Rollins does."

Juliet shook her head. "Oh, it'll be different after they get married. Mr. Tanner's a nice man. You'll have a family now—a mom and a dad and a brother and everything."

"I guess that will be nice," Jenny said quietly.

"And just think. It was my idea for them to get married."

Jenny stared at her friend. "What do you mean, your idea?"

"Oh, I knew your mother liked him and he liked her."

Jenny laughed aloud. "You're always trying to manage everything, Juliet Jones! I think instead of Too Smart Jones they ought to call you Managing Jones."

"Don't ever let anybody hear you say that!" Juliet said sharply. "That's all Billy Rollins would want—another nickname to tack on me. Well, let's go to Delores's house. And don't worry about Jack. You'll have a fine time after your mom and Mr. Tanner get married."

As they walked along toward the Del Rio house, Juliet saw that many houses were decorated for Halloween. There were carved pumpkins in front of the Williams house. Other places had orange jack-o'-lanterns around their porches. Still others had black witches, white skeletons, bats, and spiders. Some even had things that looked like tombstones in their yards.

"I don't really think Halloween's very nice," Juliet said.

"I don't much like it. I don't like to think about things like witches and bats. Mom says that we shouldn't ever pay special attention to things like that."

"That's what *my* mom and dad say."

"Anyway, we don't have to worry about

Halloween. We're going to have the greatest scavenger hunt ever. Remember last year?"

"I sure do. We were on the same team. And the hardest thing to find was a pair of old-fashioned earrings—the kind that has screws in them."

The two girls were so busy talking that Juliet did not pay much attention to anything else. Suddenly hands fell on her neck, and someone screamed right in her ear. Both Juliet and Jenny jumped and yelled.

Juliet turned around with her mouth open and saw Delores Del Rio, laughing.

"Delores, don't you ever do that again! You scared me half to death!"

"I couldn't help it. You two were so busy talking, you never even saw me. I just couldn't help myself. Where are you going?"

"Well, if I get over my scare," Juliet said, "we were going to your house to see if we could play dress up."

"That would be so much fun," Jenny said. "Do you think your grandmother would mind?"

"She says to bring you anytime you want to come. Why don't we ask if we can have a sleepover at my house? We can play dress up and have tea parties and everything else up in the attic."

"That's great!" Juliet said. "I'm glad I thought of it."

Jenny laughed. "You didn't think of it. Delores thought of it."

"Whatever! It sounds good." Juliet grabbed the hands of the other girls and said, "Let's go. And before we go to your house, let's stop at the ice cream parlor and get some ice cream."

But Jenny said, "I don't have any money."

"I do," Juliet said. "A little. At least enough for a cone apiece. No banana splits, though."

The three girls went into the ice cream parlor and started to pick out their flavors. It took a long time. Juliet finally settled on black walnut. Delores chose rocky road. And Jenny, as always, chose pecan praline. They left the shop, licking their cones.

Jenny said, "Ice cream is for summer. It's crazy eating ice cream at Halloween."

"Ice cream is good anytime," Juliet said.

As they went on down the street, Delores said, "right here A man stopped me a while ago. He asked me if I'd seen a black dog. He said his little boy lost one. He said he ran away."

"Oh yes!" Jenny said. "I heard about him. The man was going up and down all the streets looking for a black dog."

"It is sad to lose your pet," Delores said. Then she looked over at Juliet. "What are you looking so funny about, Juliet?"

Juliet said slowly, "I saw an old man out

in the woods when Joe and I were collecting leaves. An old man with a dog. I just thought about him when you mentioned a lost dog."

"What kind of an old man?"

Juliet told the story, then said, "I saw him here in town one time with his brown dog."

Jenny said. "An old man out walking his dog in the woods—nothing special about that."

The three girls went on to the Del Rio house. For the next hour and a half they played dress up. Once more they tried on all the old dresses that were in the trunk in the Del Rio attic. It was great fun.

But all the time Juliet was thinking, *Hm. Now a black dog is missing. I think the mystery begins to deepen.*

5

Another Dog

Being homeschooled had its problems. Juliet had found that out. One problem was not being around other children a lot. That was not a problem in public school. It certainly was when you studied at home and your mother was your main teacher.

But Mr. and Mrs. Jones had found out that many other parents in and around Oakwood also homeschooled their children. These families had gotten together in what they called the "Oakwood support group." Mothers and fathers who were especially good in one subject helped other people's children who had trouble with that subject. Sometimes parents and children planned schoolwork in their meetings. Sometimes they met for fun times, such as picnics and barbecues and ball games.

So it was that, one rainy Thursday afternoon,

the Oakwood support group met. Many could not come that day, but six families were there. And that was enough to have a good meeting.

The first part of the meeting was given over to showing projects done by the different students. Juliet tried to wait patiently. When their turn came, she and Joe both stood up with their display of mounted leaves. Juliet let Joe do most of the talking. He pointed out, for instance, that one leaf had "serrated" edges. That sounded very scientific.

When they finished, people clapped. Mrs. Boyd, the lady who was in charge of the meeting, complimented them both.

Billy Rollins was next. He had made a model of an oil well. Juliet thought it was not a very good one. But he went on and on and on, talking about how it worked.

After a long time, Mrs. Boyd said, "Billy, we're going to have to ask you to end your demonstration now."

Billy grew red in the face. It was clear that he didn't like to be corrected. "You didn't make Joe and Too Smart Jones stop *their* report!"

"Billy, we'll not call people names!"

"Well, you didn't!" he said loudly. "You gave them all the time they wanted."

But Mrs. Boyd shook her head firmly. "They used only nine minutes. You've been talking about oil for nearly twenty. We appreciate your work, Billy, but that's enough now."

"Well, it's not fair!" Billy Rollins stalked back to his seat and plumped himself down. He nudged Jack Tanner in the ribs and muttered, "Did you see how she cut me off?"

"I'm glad she did!" Jack muttered back. "You were boring me to death. Hey, that was a good joke. Boring oil—boring me to death. Do you get it?"

When the boys began to wrestle, Mr. Boyd stood up. "That'll be enough out of you two! I want to hear the rest of the reports."

Mr. Boyd wanted to hear because his own children, the twins Helen and Ray, were to give their report next. They had collected samples of rocks. Now they held them up, one at a time, giving their names.

Juliet overheard Flash Gordon whisper to Chili Williams, who was sitting next to him, "I'd like to have some of those rocks and a slingshot."

"After we get out of here," Chili whispered back, "we'll try that. We'll make us some slingshots."

These two were quieted down, too, and finally the schoolwork part of the meeting ended.

"Time for refreshments," Mrs. White said. She was very pretty that afternoon in a white skirt and a blue blouse. And she was extragood at planning refreshments.

"I'm glad Mrs. White's doing the food," Joe said. "Every time Mrs. Boyd does it, she brings

45

those old hard cookies that she makes. Oooh, they're awful! We could use them for paperweights."

Juliet said, "I hope Mrs. White has made another one of those pineapple cakes."

It turned out that Mrs. White *had* brought a pineapple cake. There was also a caramel cake, four different kinds of cookies, and all sorts of chips and dips. The boys and girls had a great time eating.

But since it had been raining, it looked as if they could not go outside and play afterward. So after the snacks, Mrs. Boyd called them together. She was such a fussy lady, Juliet thought. And she always liked to run things.

"Let me have your attention," Mrs. Boyd said. "I want to talk to you about the scavenger hunt we're going to have."

That excited everybody. Mrs. Boyd tried to talk, but the boys and girls were too noisy.

Finally Mr. Tanner said, "I see the rain's stopped now. Why don't you just let them go outside and play, and *we'll* do the planning?"

That suited all of the students! They ran out at once and began playing games on the wet grass. Jack Tanner and Flash Gordon began a basket-shooting contest. Flash, though he was in a wheelchair, beat him every time.

Back in the meeting room, the grown-ups were talking. First, they took care of some school business. When that was finished, Juliet's father said, "Do any of you have a dog that's been missing?"

"Not us," Mr. Boyd said. "Why would you ask that?" He was short and fat with a round face. He was the richest man in the group. And he was like his wife—he liked to run things.

"Well, I've heard people say that several dogs have been reported missing," Mr. Jones said.

"Yes. I have heard that, too." The speaker was Mr. Del Rio. He was a small, older man. He had beautiful silver hair and dark eyes. "A family down the road from us—they said one of their dogs is missing. But they have so many, I don't see how they can tell."

"Well, if the dog owners would just keep them on leashes," Mrs. Boyd said, "they wouldn't lose them!"

"I don't think the people down the street have that many leashes," Mr. Del Rio said. "They must have ten dogs."

"Then they wouldn't even care about missing one," she said.

But Mr. Tanner shook his head. It seemed he did not agree. "I think anytime anybody loses a pet, they're going to be sad about it."

Harold Rollins, Billy's father, had come in late. But right away he said what he thought. "Oh, dogs are always running off. That's all it means. We don't have time to talk about dogs. We've got plans to make for the children's scavenger hunt."

Outside, some of the boys and girls were standing around and talking about what they wanted to be when they grew up.

Billy Rollins, the loudest of the group, said, "When I grow up, I'm going to be the richest guy in the whole world!"

"I can't stand him *now*," Joe whispered to Flash, who was standing next to him. "Imagine if he had a lot of money."

"I'm going to have a different Cadillac for every day in the week," Billy said. "And I'll have all the Nintendo games there are. And maybe I'll give you all jobs. You can all work for me when I get grown up."

"That'll be the day," Joe said. "I'm not going to work for *you*. Ever!"

Jack Tanner said, "I'm gonna be a football player. Some of them make a million dollars. Wouldn't that be something—to get paid just for playing ball?"

Chili said, "Tell you what I'm going to do. I'm gonna go back to Africa and be a king over there. After we looked up our family tree, I decided it wouldn't be too bad being a king."

"What do you want to be, Jenny?" Juliet asked.

"I'd like to be like Cinderella."

"What does that mean?" Ray Boyd asked.

"Oh, it means that I'd like to have something magical happen to me, just like in the Cinderella story."

"Not me," Helen said. "I'm going to be a fashion model."

"You're too big for that," Billy Rollins said rudely. "Maybe you could be a professional wrestler."

Juliet thought it was unkind of Billy to say that. "I think it would be nice to be a fashion model, Helen."

"What do you want to be, Too Smart Jones?" Billy asked then. He reached over and gave her hair a pull.

Juliet slapped his hand. "Stop pulling my hair!"

"Well, come on. Tell us what you want to be." Billy rolled his eyes. "I'll bet you don't even know."

All the boys and girls waited to hear what Juliet would say. Most of them acted surprised when she said, "I really *don't* know what I want to be. Yet. Maybe a detective or somebody like that."

"How do you like that?" Ray Boyd jeered. "Too Smart Jones doesn't even know what she wants to be."

"Well, I'm only ten years old," Juliet said. "I don't have to know *today*."

Billy Rollins and Ray Boyd began to tease Juliet then, and soon Jack Tanner joined in.

Juliet glared at the three of them. "I don't have to tell you what I'm going to be!" She turned and walked off.

As Juliet left the crowd of boys and girls, she expected Delores and Jenny to come with her. But they did not, and that hurt her feelings. She muttered, "I don't see why they *want* to stay with those boys. That bunch just likes to make fun of people."

But, as usual, Juliet did not remain upset for long. She began thinking about what she did want to do. She had once thought she would like to be a doctor. Another time, she thought maybe she might become a jet pilot. Or a detective like Sherlock Holmes. But she really did not know.

And then Juliet saw something that made her eyes fly open. A small, scruffy brown dog suddenly appeared down the street. And then the same little old man that she and Joe had seen in the woods came around a corner.

Juliet could hardly breathe. "It's him," she said out loud. "And he's got *another* dog with him!" The second dog with the strange man was large and black.

Juliet ran back to where Jenny White was on a swing. "Come look down the street, Jenny," she said. "I saw him. It's the man I saw in the woods. The man we saw in town that night."

Others were standing around the swings. They wanted to know *what* man.

"It's just a . . . a stranger I saw out in the woods. There's something mysterious about him."

As usual, anytime Juliet said anything, Billy Rollins acted as if it wasn't important. He looked down the street. "So what if he's a stranger in town? You have to make a mystery out of every-thing, Too Smart!"

"Yeah." Ray Boyd laughed. "Maybe you ought to go and find out who he is. Maybe he'll kidnap you, and we'd be rid of you once and for all."

The mean teasing went on for some time, but Juliet did not really listen. She kept think-ing about the man. Then she just walked away.

Joe followed her. "It *is* the same old man, isn't it?" he said.

"Yes, it is. And the same brown dog. But he's got a *black* dog with him this time, too. Joe, I heard that somebody was looking for a lost black dog!"

Joe looked after the old man and the dogs as they disappeared down the street. Then he said, "It sure looks like there's a mystery to solve this time."

6

Adventure in the Woods

Juliet worked on her studies all the next day. When she finally finished them all and had done her homework and her chores, she said, "Mom, I'm going out for a walk. OK?"

"All right. Just be sure you're home in time for supper."

"I will, Mom."

As Juliet went down the street, she began to ask everyone she saw, "Have you seen a strange old man with a brown dog? Or a black dog?"

No one had, however, and most of the people didn't even seem interested. Juliet was disgusted. *Don't they know there's a mystery here?* she said to herself.

Then she saw Mr. Sands across the street. Mr. Sands was an older man, who walked with a cane. Juliet had always liked him. She ran over and said, "Hello, Mr. Sands."

"Why, hello, Juliet. I haven't seen you in a long time. How have you been?"

"I'm fine. How have you been?"

"A few aches and pains, but I'm all right." Mr. Sands had a kind face. He grinned down at her and asked, "What are you up to today?"

"I've been trying to find out something about a man that I saw."

"What's his name?"

"I don't know his name. I've only seen him three times." Juliet described the man that she had seen the best she could. "And every time, he's had a little brown dog with him. The last time, he had a black dog with him, too."

"Well," Mr. Sands said, "that sounds a whole lot like a fellow I know."

"You know him?" Juliet said with excitement.

"I'm not sure. But from what you say, it does sound like him."

"What's his name?"

"His name is Liles. James Liles."

"Where does he live?"

"I'm not sure anymore. I don't get around much these days."

"But you know something about him?"

"If it's Liles, I know he lives alone. He hardly ever goes anywhere. Is kind of a hermit—if it's the same man."

"Why is he a hermit?"

Mr. Sands rubbed his chin thoughtfully. "I

don't really know why, but he is. We went to school together a long, long time ago."

"You mean before I was born?"

Mr. Sands laughed quietly. "I mean before your mother and father were born."

"Wow! That was a long time ago!"

"Yes, it was. And I think about those days a lot. Anyway, he grew up and moved away. I didn't see him for years, Juliet. I grew up, too, and married and had my family and my grandchildren. And then—it must have been about five years ago—James Liles showed up again."

"Where had he been all those years?"

"He never did say."

Juliet thought hard, then asked, "But *why* does he keep to himself?"

"Like I said, I don't know, Juliet. I've only seen him two or three times since he moved back here. I just know I once asked him to come and visit with me, but he never would. He didn't want to be very sociable for some reason."

"What's he like, Mr. Sands? I mean, what kind of a man is he?"

Mr. Sands sighed. "Well, he's not mean or anything like that. He just seems kind of . . . sad."

Juliet talked to Mr. Sands a while longer, but she did not learn much more about the strange man.

Mr. Sands finally said, "I know that he used

to live over on the northeast side of the woods —in a house that at one time belonged to a family called Johnson. But that's all I know."

"Well, thank you anyway, Mr. Sands."

"Good-bye, Juliet."

Juliet decided to walk to the woods and see if she could find Mr. Liles's house. She had not gone far, however, when suddenly the toe of her Keds caught in a crack in the sidewalk, and down she went.

"Ow, that hurt!" she said. She found a Kleenex in her pocket and dabbed at her knee. Then she got up and went on. She had a mystery to solve.

When she got to the edge of the woods, for some reason the forest seemed a little scary today. But she straightened up and said loudly, "I'm not afraid of any old woods!"

She began walking slowly along the trail that was made for bikes. She was really getting frightened, although she would not admit it. She was relieved when she saw Flash Gordon wheeling himself toward her.

"Hi, Juliet. You need a ride?"

"No, thank you," Juliet said.

"What's the matter?" Flash asked. He wheeled along beside her and looked up into her face. "You look worried."

"If I tell you, you'll just think I'm stupid."

"Aw, you can tell me anything. I know you're not stupid."

"All right, then. I will." Juliet told Flash about the man and the dogs and what was bothering her.

Immediately he said, "Hey, I'd like to help solve a mystery! I'll just go along with you."

"That would be nice. I was maybe going to go back and get Joe to come with me."

"OK. We'll get him too."

An hour later, Juliet, Joe, and Flash were making their way through the woods. They had chosen the bike path again, so that Flash's wheelchair could go through. Sometimes he pushed himself, but usually Juliet or Joe shoved his chair along.

Once when Juliet was doing the pushing, Joe ran way ahead.

Juliet yelled after him, "Slow down, Joe! Don't run off and leave us."

He came back, but he said, "I'm in charge this time. And we're not going to leave any paper trail, either. I've got my compass." He fished the compass out of his backpack and studied it carefully.

Juliet said, "We have to get to the northeast corner of the woods."

"OK. That's all we need to know," Joe said, and he started off.

Juliet lost sight of him more than once. "He's doing that on purpose," she told Flash.

"He always likes to run away and hide behind trees and bushes just to scare me."

After they'd walked for a while, they came to the stream that ran through the middle of the woods. It was shallow, but Juliet knew it was cold. They didn't want to get their feet wet, so they looked around until they found a log they could walk across.

"But you can't cross on that log on your chair, Flash," Juliet said, frowning.

"That's all right. I'll wait for you here. I'll be a lookout. But if you get into trouble, just holler, and I'll come splashing through."

Juliet smiled. Flash Gordon was one of the most agreeable boys she had ever met. "All right, then. You're the lookout."

Juliet and Joe carefully walked across the log. On the other side, they kept on walking, heading east. And then Juliet said, "Listen. Do you hear that?"

"Do I hear what?" Joe asked. Then he nodded. "Yeah. It's dogs barking. Come on. We've got to be Indian scouts now."

"What's that mean?"

"It means don't make so much racket! Don't step on any dry sticks or stuff and don't make any noise. Let's go."

Very slowly and carefully, Joe led the way. And then he whispered, "Look. Over there!"

Juliet looked through the trees. What she saw was a small, well-kept house sitting back in a clearing in the dense woods. She also saw on the front porch a small, scruffy brown dog.

Even as Juliet saw his ears perk up, the dog jumped off the porch and headed straight for them, barking wildly.

"Let's run for it!" Joe said. "He could bite!"

Juliet was truly scared now, and she turned to run. But then she saw a big black dog and a medium-sized yellow dog. And she heard still another one barking somewhere at the back of the house. "Let's get out of here—fast!" Juliet looked back one more time. She saw a man step out on the porch.

She heard the man say, "You dogs stop that barking and get back to the house!"

But the dogs didn't obey. None of them tried to bite, but they ran after Juliet and Joe until they came to the stream.

This time neither Juliet nor her brother bothered with crossing the log. They went splashing right through the water. Joe slipped and fell headlong, and Juliet was wet to the waist when they crawled out.

There sat Flash in his wheelchair, laughing. "If you two aren't a sorry sight! What did you see that made you run like that? And where'd all those dogs come from?"

"Never mind, Flash. Let's just get out of here."

Juliet started running again, and Joe followed her. Flash rolled along close behind.

The silver wheels of his chair flashed as they went down the path. The sound of barking dogs grew faint in the distance.

7

Do We
Tell the Police?

Although Juliet and Joe were scared out of their wits, Flash did not seem to be. All the time the three homeschoolers were hurrying out of the woods, Juliet knew he was laughing. From time to time he would spin his wheelchair around on two wheels.

He rolled up beside Juliet and Joe just as they came out of the trees. "You two were sure funny!" he said. "Let's go back and see if you can jump that creek again. You didn't quite make it the last time."

"Oh, quiet!" Joe said crossly. He was probably angry at himself. The cold water had soaked him. He shivered and looked at Juliet angrily, as if it were her fault. "We're going to freeze if we don't get out of these wet clothes."

Flash grinned. "Let's go back across the

creek again. Maybe they'll take you in at that house you say you saw back there."

And suddenly Juliet started laughing—even though she was cold and wet, too. She looked down at her dripping skirt. She looked at her soaked shoes. She glanced at Joe, who looked like a miserable drowned rat. Then she said between peals of laughter, "I guess we did look pretty funny, sailing out of the woods like that."

Joe glared at her for a moment. But soon he began to grin, too. And then he shrugged his shoulders. "I'll have to take lessons in jumping creeks, I guess. *Brrrr*, it's cold!"

Flash grew serious then. "Let's get you two home. You're going to catch cold out here."

"I think you're right about that," Juliet said.

"What all did you see over there?" Flash asked as they hurried along. "Did you solve the mystery yet?"

"Not yet," Juliet said. "There was that house, and I saw a man. But when the dogs came after us, we just lost it."

"Let's just hurry," Joe said. "We can figure it out later." He grabbed her arm, and they started to walk faster.

Flash stayed with them until they came to the cutoff to his house. "When you go on another adventure, come see me. Flash Gordon. No adventure turned down. We never close."

As Juliet and Joe hurried on toward home, Joe shook his head. "He sure is one upbeat guy."

"He really is. You'd never know that he had a problem in the world."

When Juliet and Joe got to their house, they practically fell in the front door. They were shivering and sopping wet.

Juliet had wanted to sneak in without being seen, but it was too late for that.

Their mother came out of the kitchen and stopped, staring at them. She uttered one cry of surprise. "Well, my goodness!" Then she rushed forward. "What in the world happened to you two?"

"We got wet," Joe said.

"I can see that. Did you fall in the lake? What were you doing to get like this?"

Juliet did not want to tell her mother that she had been out trying to solve a mystery. Both parents said that she was spending too much time on things like that. Quickly she said, "Well, we were out in the woods, and Joe slipped and fell into the creek . . ."

"And how did *you* get wet?" Mrs. Jones demanded.

"I guess I kind of slipped and fell in the creek myself."

Their mother frowned. "There's something funny about all this."

"It's not very funny," Joe said. "I'm freezing, Mom. Can I go get out of these wet clothes?"

"All right. But we're going to talk about this later. You two may be grounded for a week."

"Aw, Mom—"

"Don't argue with me, Joseph Jones! Now, both of you go take a hot bath and put on some warm clothes."

Joe and Juliet hurried up the stairs. Joe was muttering, "I hope we don't get grounded. That's the pits."

"I hope not, too," Juliet said. "But it's all your fault. If you hadn't fallen in the creek, no one would have ever known what we were doing."

Joe glared but didn't take time to answer. He ran into his room to strip off his wet clothes.

Juliet immediately grabbed a robe and a towel and ran to the bathroom that was between her room and Joe's. She locked the door.

Soon Joe was outside the bathroom door, calling, "Juliet, are you in there?"

"Yes, I am," she said.

"Well, hurry up!"

"I'll be as quick as I can."

"Let me take my bath first. It takes you forever."

Juliet said, "I'll hurry up! Now, go away!"

It took Juliet "forever," as Joe had said, to get out of the bathroom. Then Joe went in.

When they both were in warm clothing, they had a meeting in Juliet's room. Joe was walking back and forth, and Juliet was sitting in front of her mirror, brushing out her hair.

"This mystery's kind of getting a hold on me," Joe said.

"Me too," Juliet said. "Even though I know that some people don't really care about their missing dogs."

"Yeah. I talked to Gerald Flannigan. He lives way on the other side of town. His uncle lives right beside them. One of his uncle's dogs disappeared, but Gerald said his uncle didn't care that much. Didn't even report it to the police."

For some time Juliet and Joe talked about the missing dogs and the strange old man. At last Joe asked, "So do we tell the police about him?"

"I don't know whether we should or not. Would the police take the dogs back to their owners?"

"How would they even know which families the dogs belong to?"

They talked around in circles for a while longer.

Then Juliet said, "Well, all I can say is, we need to pray before we do anything."

"All right," Joe agreed. "We'll pray about it and see what the Lord says to do."

When Juliet and Joe's dad came home, he talked to them sternly about falling into the creek. But he did not ground them.

When Juliet prayed at bedtime, she said, "Thank You, Lord, for not letting me be grounded. And please let Joe and me know what to do about that old man and about the dogs."

After praying, she felt satisfied. "I know it's going to be all right," she said aloud. "Somehow God is going to help me solve this mystery."

She got into bed and pulled up the covers.

8

The Scavenger Hunt

The most exciting fall event for the home-schoolers was the Big Scavenger Hunt. It was the time of year when most people cele-brated Halloween. But for the Oakwood home-school group, the scavenger hunt was more suitable. For a while, some of the youngsters complained because they didn't get to go trick-or-treating. But the grown-ups worked so hard to make the scavenger hunt fun that most of the students were happy with the new activity.

"I don't miss what we used to do for Hal-loween a bit," Juliet said. She and Joe were in his room, getting ready to leave for the hunt.

Joe was searching madly for his eye patch. He was going as a pirate. Their mother had worked hard on his costume. Now he was dig-ging things out of his chest of drawers and muttering, "What did I do with that eye patch?

I need my eye patch! I can't go without an eye patch!"

Juliet went over to Joe's mirror and looked at herself. She had decided to go as Sherlock Holmes. She had watched the Sherlock Holmes TV programs, and she and her mother had worked until she had a fine costume. Juliet had on brown slacks held up by a pair of brown suspenders. She wore a white shirt buttoned up around the neck and a yellow-and-brown vest and brown shoes. And she carried a huge magnifying glass and a big pipe.

The hardest part of making the costume had been finding a "deer stalker hat" like the kind Mr. Holmes wore. Her mother had finally made one. It was a hat with bills pointing in both directions. She also made a cloak out of an old winter coat.

Juliet lifted the magnifying glass. She peered at Joe through it. It was the one they had used for their science fair. She felt as if she were the great detective himself. She waved the curved pipe at Joe. "Aha, Dr. Watson. I think we're going to solve this mystery."

At that moment Joe found his eye patch. "Here you are!" He grunted happily and took it out of the drawer. He slipped it over his head and over his eye, then grinned. "Where'd you get that pipe?"

"Mr. Ramsey next door. He let me borrow it. Phew, it smells!" Juliet made a face. But she thought the pipe was a good finishing touch to her Sherlock Holmes costume.

"Well, come on. Let's go see if Mom and Dad are ready."

They found their parents ready to go. The grown-ups were not wearing costumes, but they both admired Juliet and Joe.

"Why, you look like Bluebeard the pirate himself!" Their father grinned. "Where'd you get that sword?"

"I made it," Joe said proudly. He pulled the sword from his belt and waved it in the air.

"Look out! You'll cut someone with that thing!" his mother cried.

"No, it's just made of wood. The foil around it makes it look like it's made out of metal."

"Well, it looks real enough," Mr. Jones said. "You did a good job."

"Thanks, Dad."

"And you look like Sherlock Holmes himself, Juliet," her father said. "You girls did a good job on that costume. Hey—just a minute! That's my good coat you made that hat out of!"

"It was all worn out. You need a new one," Mrs. Jones said firmly.

"There was lots of wear left in that coat!" he complained.

"Well, it's too late now. I can't make a coat back out of her hat. Now let's go. We're going to be late for the scavenger hunt."

It was so pleasant outside that they decided to walk to the community center. But fall was turning into winter, and the evening was cool.

It was the day before Halloween. The homeschoolers had decided it would be too confusing to have a scavenger hunt at the same time that other groups were out playing trick or treat.

As Juliet and Joe and their parents walked along, many of the neighbors called out and commented on their costumes.

Mrs. Fitzgerald, who lived a few houses down the street from the Joneses, came out from where she was pulling weeds from a flower bed. "Let me look at you two," she said. She admired both costumes. Then she said, "I went to a costume party once when I was sixteen years old."

"What did you wear?" Juliet asked. She liked Mrs. Fitzgerald very much.

"I went as a Southern belle. I had a hoop skirt, and there were ribbons all over the dress. I had a big garden hat tied under my chin, and I carried a fluffy parasol."

"I'll bet you looked beautiful," Mrs. Jones said.

Mrs. Fitzgerald shrugged. "It was a beautiful dress, and I had a good time. I think costume parties are always fun."

"We'll be back to see you after a while, Mrs. Fitzgerald," Juliet said. "We're having a scavenger hunt. And sometimes the list has some pretty funny things on it. So we'll be coming to your house."

Mrs. Fitzgerald laughed. "Are you saying I keep funny things?"

As a matter of fact, Mrs. Fitzgerald did keep funny things. She never threw anything away.

One of the most interesting things in her house—at least, to Joe—was a huge stuffed moose head. He grinned at her and said, "If a moose head is on our list, you can bet we'll be back, Mrs. Fitzgerald."

The family hurried along. By the time they reached the community center, it was already humming with activity.

Mr. Rollins was in charge of the scavenger hunt. He soon called everyone together and said importantly, "All right, now! We've divided you up into groups. Each group will have a captain. And those of you who are in the group will have to do what your captain says."

"I'll bet the captain of one group will be old Billy Rollins," Joe muttered.

He was right. Group number one had five people in it. And it was captained by Billy Rollins.

Juliet and Joe were both in the third group. Mr. Rollins announced that Flash Gordon would be their captain.

"That's good," Juliet whispered. "They say

Flash is the best digger-upper of stuff than anybody. His group won last year."

"We're going to win this time too," Joe said.

The prize, Juliet knew, was a trip to Six Flags.

Jenny and Chili Williams hurried over to be with Flash's group, too. Chili grinned and said, "We're going to win the prize. Isn't that right, Juliet? You're the one who's so smart, so you ought to know."

Juliet ignored his teasing. She turned to Flash. "We're going to do our best, Flash. You just tell us what to do."

Mr. Rollins's voice rose again above all the chatter. "Listen, now. I have the list of items here. We're going to hand them out to your captains. Don't open them until I say go." Then Mr. Rollins gave a list to each group.

Flash took their sheet of paper. As soon as Mr. Rollins said, "All right—go!" Flash said, "Let's get out of here."

Outside the community building, Flash stopped. There was still enough light to see by. He held up the list and said, "The first thing we're going to do is organize. We won't all look for the same things. See. There are twenty things to find. We'll split up and go two and two."

"But there are *five* of us!"

"Juliet, you go by yourself. The rest of us

will pair off. Now, here." He tore the list into three pieces. "Get this stuff and get back as quick as you can."

Juliet studied her list. Then she said, "Oh boy! I know where three of these things are right now." She dashed off to start her search.

On Juliet's list was a silver bell. She knew Mrs. Fitzgerald had one. Juliet had seen it on a table.

Another item was a toy that was at least thirty years old. "That'll be easy," Juliet said. Joe had a little army tank that wound up and went crawling around on rubber treads. It had belonged to their dad.

The third item that she knew she could get was one ski. There was nowhere to ski around Oakwood. But she knew that Darrell Jenkins, who lived two streets over from her, went to Colorado to ski every year. *He won't mind letting me borrow one of his skis,* she thought.

Soon Juliet had collected all of the easy items. It took her a while to find a license plate from another state. Finally she remembered an old barn at the edge of town. It had all kinds of old license plates nailed on the door. They were rusty, but the rules didn't say that the license plate had to be pretty. She found one from the state of Mississippi and then began looking for the final item.

She read it again. "Something from World War One." She could not for the life of her think of where to get that. There was a small museum in Oakwood that had a rifle from World War One. But she couldn't borrow that.

Then Juliet came to the drugstore. It was still open, and she ran in to get a drink of water. The druggist, Mr. Justice, asked, "And what are you doing with all that stuff, Juliet?"

"It's for our scavenger hunt."

Mr. Justice was a tall man with gray hair and kindly blue eyes. "I used to enjoy those a lot. You got all the things?"

"All except one," she said.

"What's missing?"

"Something from World War One. It's easy to get stuff from World War Two. But World War One was a long time ago."

Mr. Justice looked at Juliet for a moment. Then he nodded his head. "I think I can help you out, young lady." He disappeared behind the counter where he mixed prescriptions. Soon he came out with a small wooden box. "How about this?"

Juliet opened it. There was a medal inside. "Is this from World War One?"

"It is, and it belonged to my great-uncle. I've kept it all these years. He was very kind to me."

Juliet looked down at the medal, then up at Mr. Justice. "Do you think I might borrow it? I'll be very careful with it."

"I'm sure Uncle Henry would be happy to

have a fine young lady like you use his medal. Just be careful with it."

"I will," Juliet said quickly. She grabbed up all of the items that she had collected and hurried out of the store.

Flash and Chili were already at the community building. "Have you got everything on your list?" Flash asked.

"Yes!"

"That's good. We have our stuff, too. Joe and Jenny aren't back yet."

"There they are now!" Juliet pointed. Then she yelled to the newcomers, "Do you have it all?"

"We have it. Every bit!" Jenny said. Her eyes flashed with excitement. Joe was carrying some heavy items, and she clutched a paper sack.

"Let's check in before somebody else shows up," Flash said.

They hurried inside, and the grown-ups looked up with surprise.

"Surely you don't have *everything* on that list!" Mr. Rollins said. He looked disappointed. Maybe he'd hoped that his son's team would win.

"We have everything!"

"We'll have to check over the items very carefully," Mr. Rollins said.

Mr. Rollins did, indeed, check everything very carefully. He had a question about almost every item.

But finally Mr. Tanner said, "I'd say this group has won, fair and square. The rest of them still aren't in sight."

Mr. Rollins grumbled, but there was nothing he could do.

"How did you find things so quickly?" Mrs. Del Rio asked.

"Flash divided us up. Instead of all of us looking for everything, we went out two by two. Well, two by two and one," Juliet said.

Mrs. Del Rio smiled. "I bet you thought up that idea, didn't you?"

"It was Flash who thought of it. He was the captain."

"Well, I think it's very fine."

"Are you disappointed that Samuel and Delores didn't win?" Juliet asked.

"No, it's their first year. Maybe they'll win next year."

The teams kept straggling in. It was two hours before they were all back. There was a lot of laughter about some of the things they'd found. Only the Boyd twins and Billy Rollins complained.

"I bet Juliet Jones cheated somehow," Billy muttered.

"Nope. She didn't." Flash grinned. "Come on. Take it like a man, Billy."

Billy Rollins seemed to feel better about the scavenger hunt when they got to sit down and have refreshments. The parents had brought salads and dips and sandwiches and—best of all—desserts. There were pudding cups with cookie crumbs on top to look like dirt—and with candy worms sticking out of them. There were cookies decorated as pumpkins. There were cupcakes with bright orange frosting and candy on top. There were little fruit tarts, and one of Mrs. White's famous pineapple cakes, and sweet-tasting orange punch.

When the party broke up, Juliet told her father about how she found the medal from World War One.

"Mr. Justice is very proud of it."

"He should be," Mr. Jones said. "We need to honor the men and women who served our country."

"I'm going to take the medal back in the morning. And he's going to tell me all about what his uncle did to earn it."

"Maybe you could make a report on that for your next school assignment," her mother said.

Juliet's eyes brightened. "That's what I'll do!"

That night Juliet was almost asleep before she remembered the man and the missing dog.

"Well, I forgot about solving a mystery for one night, anyhow," she said out loud. "But I bet I'll be thinking about it tomorrow morning."

9

Too Much Imagination

For several days after the scavenger hunt, Joe and Juliet worked hard on their studies. They were already thinking about Christmas.

Juliet said, "I want to get all of our projects finished so I don't have to think about them at all at Christmas time."

For once, Joe agreed with her.

The walls of the room they used as a classroom were covered with maps and charts and pictures. Juliet and Joe each had a desk. Another desk held a computer—which they often argued over, for both loved to work on it.

They kept old projects until the room got too crowded to work in it. Then their mother would insist that they be stored away. Juliet never wanted to throw out anything, so the storage shed in back of the house was getting full.

Their father walked in. He looked at the

two of them hard at work and said, "I don't believe these are my children. Joe, are you sure you don't want to take a break?"

Joe looked up from his project. He was building a model of the Eiffel Tower. It was still only half finished. "No, Dad. I've got to finish this."

Mr. Jones walked over and studied the tower. "That's a great piece of work you're doing there."

"Well, it's fun to make something and get a break from books!"

Juliet looked up from the book she was reading. She was wearing her black horn-rimmed glasses. "Dad, did you know that America wouldn't have won the Revolution if it hadn't been for France?"

"Really?" Mr. Jones said. "How did that come about?"

"Well," Juliet said. "It says here that England and France were always having wars. So when the American colonies declared their independence, France helped us."

"How did France help?"

"Well, there was an actor over there. His name was Beaumarches. And he was sort of a secret agent. He shipped muskets and gunpowder and all kinds of supplies to George Washington's army."

"I didn't know about him," their father said.

"That's right, Dad." Joe looked up from his

model. "The problem was, every time George Washington's army won a battle, the British would just back up to the seacoast."

"And you know what was behind them?" Juliet broke in. "The whole British navy."

Joe nodded. "And they couldn't fight against the big guns on the ships."

"So what happened?" Mr. Jones seemed pleased that his children were learning such things.

"What happened was that France sent *their* navy over. And they drove the British navy off. It was really the first time the French ever beat the English at sea," Juliet said.

"So General Cornwallis had to give up. Look, I have a picture of him surrendering." Joe jumped up and ruffled through a history book. "See. There's General Washington."

"So that's the way it was," Juliet said. "We could beat the British army because the French helped."

"Well, you'll have to tell me more about this later. You two *sure* you don't want to take time out?"

"No. We're going to finish our projects by Christmas, Dad," Juliet told him. "Then I'm not going to even look at a book until we start school again."

The following night, Juliet and Joe did take time out to go shopping with their parents.

They went to the department store. And there they found some of the other boys and girls from their homeschool group.

After the shopping was done, the parents went to have coffee. All the students walked down the street toward the ice cream parlor.

As they were on their way, Billy Rollins said, "How's Too Smart Jones today? You solved any mysteries?"

Juliet tried to ignore Billy. She lagged behind to get away from him. Then she stopped to look in a shop window that had a dress she liked. Just as she started to catch up again, she glanced down a side street. Down about a block, she saw something in the streetlights.

Juliet squinted into the darkness. She caught her breath. "It's him!"

She was almost sure it was the old man—and following him were five or six dogs!

"I know it's him!" She did not know what to do. She started down the side street toward him. She strained her eyes, for the old man was walking away. "But none of those dogs are on leashes," she muttered. "They're just following him. Why would dogs do that if they weren't *his* dogs? And why would he want to steal dogs and then bring them to town?"

Juliet was sure these were the stolen dogs. But she could not think of why anyone would want to steal them. She knew that some dogs were worth a lot of money—such as hunting dogs or show dogs. But none of the dogs that had disappeared were special. It was a mystery indeed for Too Smart Jones.

"He must have stolen them for some other reason." She stood there watching him go. And then she saw her father and mother coming along from the coffee shop.

"Dad," she cried. "Look down there!"

Mr. Jones stopped. "What did you say?"

"Look down there! Down Maple Street!"

Her mom and dad both looked. "So what?"

"Don't you see them?" Juliet cried.

"I don't see anything. What are you talking about?" Mrs. Jones asked.

Juliet turned and saw that now there was nothing to see. The old man and the dogs had disappeared.

"Juliet, I think your imagination's getting out of hand. You always did have a little bit too much imagination," her mother said.

"What was it you thought you saw?" Mr. Jones asked curiously.

Juliet did not want to tell. She was sure that her parents would scold her for trying to solve another mystery. And she didn't want anyone, especially her father, to think that she just imagined things.

"Oh, nothing, I guess. Let's go find Joe. There he is—up with the other kids."

Juliet walked along with her parents. She was thinking, *I know that was the old man.*

And I know that those were the stolen dogs. She thought about going back. But she knew that her parents would never permit that. It was already getting late.

Well, I know what I saw, and that's that.

She said nothing more to anyone, not even to Joe. As they went on home, though, Juliet made up her mind to somehow find out more about the old man and those mysterious missing dogs.

10

A Broken Heart

Juliet had always loved mysteries. But one Tuesday afternoon, the case of the missing dogs *really* became important to her.

She had gone to visit Jenny White. The girls spent the afternoon playing with Jenny's large collection of Barbie dolls. Jenny had named every one of them. She knew them as well as if they were real people. But she always seemed surprised at how well Juliet remembered them.

"I play with them every day," Jenny said. "That's how I remember them. But I don't see how *you* can keep them straight."

Juliet never stopped to think about how she remembered things. Remembering was easy for her. At times she wished she were better at doing things with her hands. Or that she could sing as well as Jenny could. Or do some of the things that other people did better.

"People talk about me being smart, but I'd rather be able to sing like you, Jenny. You have such a pretty voice."

Jenny shrugged her shoulders. "Well, they don't give good grades for that."

"But you can entertain people. Who wants to sit around and watch me do arithmetic problems?"

Jenny laughed. "That wouldn't be much of a show, would it?"

"Well, I've got to go home. See you tomorrow. Are you still coming over for our sleepover?"

"Mom said I could. And I'll bring some of my dolls."

"OK." Juliet knew that they would never get to play with the dolls. They would be doing other things. But Jenny liked to take some Barbies everywhere she went.

Juliet said good-bye to Jenny and her mother. She left their house and started walking down the street. She had her small Walkman radio and was listening to Christian music. She sang along, for she knew the words to all the songs. She knew she couldn't sing as well as Jenny, but she liked to sing, anyway.

She crossed Third Street and turned down toward her neighborhood. And then she saw a little girl sitting on the curb. She looked to be about five years old. She seemed to be troubled about something.

Juliet walked over to her and said, "Is anything wrong?"

The little girl looked up. "Yes," she said. Then she burst out crying.

Juliet sat down on the curb beside her. "What's your name? I'm Juliet Jones."

The little girl was crying so hard she couldn't talk. Finally she choked it out. "Abigail."

"Well, Abigail, what's wrong? Did you fall down and hurt yourself?"

"No."

"Did you do something naughty and get fussed at by your mother?"

"No."

"Well, why don't you tell me what it was? Maybe I can help."

"No, you can't help. Nobody can help."

The little girl was very pretty. She had blonde curly hair and big blue eyes. There was a little dirt on her face where she had been rubbing her eyes. And she looked as sorrowful as any child that Juliet had ever seen.

"Come on now, Abigail. Tell me. You never know. I might be able to help."

"It's Noodles."

"Noodles."

"Yes. It's Noodles."

"You don't like noodles?"

"I love Noodles."

"Then why are you crying?"

"Because he's lost."

Suddenly Juliet understood. Abigail was not talking about the noodles that you eat for supper. She was talking about a pet.

"Is Noodles your kitten?"

"No. My doggie."

Juliet sat up straighter. *Another lost dog!* she thought. "When did you lose him?"

"Just yesterday. My daddy and my mommy looked everywhere, and so did I. But we can't find him."

"What does Noodles look like?"

"He's the prettiest puppy ever."

"I know that," Juliet said. "But is he black or white? Does he have long hair or short hair?"

"He has lots of hair. And it gets in his face sometimes. And he's the best doggie in the whole world."

Then Juliet was aware that someone had come up behind them. She looked around to see a woman standing there. "Hello," she said quickly. "Abigail was just telling me about Noodles."

"Yes, it's sad. She loved that dog."

Juliet stood and said, "I'm Juliet Jones. We live down the street."

"I'm Mrs. Harrington." The woman had a worried look on her face. "I don't know what we're going to do. Abigail couldn't even go to sleep last night."

"Why don't you tell me what the dog looks like? I'll have all my friends look for him."

"Oh, that would be very helpful. We've told the police, but no one really cares about a missing puppy."

She described the dog. It was a medium-sized terrier. It was white. It had a fuzzy face. "If you find him, please bring him back. Abigail's heart is broken."

Juliet leaned over and said, "Don't you worry, Abigail. We'll find him."

"Do you really think so?"

"I think so. We'll just ask the Lord to help us."

Abigail tried to smile.

Juliet nodded to Abigail's mother. "We'll start looking right away."

She ran toward home. The mystery of the missing dogs suddenly seemed more important now. Solving it had been just a sort of game before. But now she kept thinking of Abigail, crying her heart out over a missing dog.

And there's no telling how many kids are missing their dogs. I'm going to find out what's going on. And now I know exactly what to do.

11

The Old
Man's Story

As soon as Juliet woke up, she remembered the promise she had made to herself. She would do *something* about Abigail's missing dog.

For a while she lay in bed thinking of all that had gone on. It seemed to her that the case of the missing dogs had built up slowly. At first it did not appear very important. Later, the case seemed perhaps just important enough to work on. But after meeting little Abigail yesterday—who was crying over the loss of her pet—Juliet made up her mind that something had to be done right away.

She got up then and went to the bathroom to wash her face and comb her hair. Then she went back to her bedroom to dress. It was still early. She could hear no sounds in the house. She liked to get up early like this. Joe always liked to sleep as late as possible. But the early morning hours were what Juliet really enjoyed.

She put on a pair of old jeans, a red-and-white sweater set, some white socks, and her favorite white Keds. Then she sat down in front of her window. The wind was blowing the leaves that had fallen from the trees. She could hear their rustling sound as they danced across the yard. She knew that before long she would be able to smell leaves burning. And that was one of the things she most enjoyed about the fall.

Juliet picked up her Bible and began to read. She liked to read in the Psalms, and for a while she read some here and there. But finally she settled on the Twenty-third Psalm, which was one of her favorites.

She read the psalm slowly and thought about what it said. Afterwards she closed her Bible and sat awhile praying, first for her family and then for her friends in the homeschool support group. At the end, Juliet prayed a special prayer. "Lord, help me to find Abigail's dog. She's lonely, and she's sad, and she needs Noodles back. I know You can do it, Jesus, so I'm asking You to help me know what to do."

By this time she could hear her mother downstairs making noise in the kitchen. Juliet knew what she was doing, and she went down to help her.

"Mom, can I help you make breakfast?"

"Of course you can. Why don't you start the oatmeal?"

Making oatmeal was easy. Juliet took a large pan out of the cupboard. She measured two cups of water and poured them into the pan. She added a little salt. Then she put the pan on the stove. When the water started to boil, Juliet added a cup of oatmeal and turned down the heat. She stirred it once. And then she turned off the heat and put a lid on the pan. The oatmeal was ready.

Next, her mother let her put butter on the toast.

By the time breakfast was on the table, her dad and Joe were both downstairs. Soon they were all seated.

"What are you up to today, Juliet?" her father asked after he'd thanked God for the food. He took a bite of buttered toast and smiled at her. "You got a big case you're working on?"

Juliet bit her lip. "Well, just something I'm interested in," she said.

"Uh-oh. I know what that means!" her mother said. "When you are 'working on a case,' you are always interested in it. What is it this time?"

"It's about those missing dogs. That's what it is," Joe said.

"Joe, be quiet!" Juliet snapped.

"Well, it is, isn't it?" he demanded. "That's all you think about. I can tell."

Juliet put down her spoonful of oatmeal. "Well, I think the thing about these missing dogs is just too bad!" And she told the story of Abigail and her lost dog. "She's really sad, and I'd like to help her find it."

"I must say that's a good thing to try to do," Mr. Jones said quietly. "Have you prayed about how to help? Praying first is always a good idea."

"Yes, I have, Dad. And I think God's going to help me find the answer to all of this."

"Why don't we all just pray about it?"

The four of them held hands, and Mr. Jones prayed quietly that God would help Juliet know what to do.

After their dad said, "Amen," Joe said, "Well, OK. That takes care of that."

"I hope so," Juliet said. "I'd really, really like to help people get their dogs back."

As usual, Juliet and Joe spent the morning working on their schoolwork. In the afternoon, they took time out to go down to the playground for a while.

But Joe soon decided to go home. He said he wanted to go back and work on a new invention. He tried to explain it to Juliet, but it didn't make any sense to her. It had something to do with turning lights on and off.

After her brother left, Juliet thought she would walk for a while in the park. She went over to the woods, got on the bike path, and headed northeast.

The sun was not bright. The sky was clouded over. But Juliet was not afraid in the shadowy woods today. She was thinking of how she had prayed about helping people find their lost dogs.

One time, a deer suddenly leaped across the bike path and disappeared into the woods. She watched the beautiful animal go bounding away. "Oh, that's the prettiest thing in the world!" Juliet breathed. "I don't see how anyone could shoot a beautiful creature like that."

And then she was at the stream where she and Joe had fallen in a few days earlier. She stood looking down at it. She could see a mass of small, silvery minnows above the sandy bottom. They stayed very still for a while, and then suddenly all shot away in a group. It was as if they were blown by a strong wind.

And just as suddenly Juliet said, "I'm going to go to that house and talk to that old man."

She found the log that she and Joe had crossed on. She went across it today without any problem. She expected to feel afraid as she got closer to the house. But she didn't—even though it was much darker among the trees than the last time. She had the feeling that everything was going to work out just fine.

After a while she heard a dog barking. Other dogs joined in with it. And then she came in sight of the house.

Sure enough, there was the whole pack of dogs. The first one she saw was the scruffy brown dog that was always with the old man. She remembered how the dogs had chased Joe and her the last time, but none of them had tried to bite. She kept on walking. The dogs started toward her, but she did not stop.

Soon Juliet was surrounded by dogs. They were all yapping. Some of them were jumping up. But that was all. The scruffy brown dog, especially, pushed close, and she patted his head. Then she noticed another dog, and her heart leaped. "That's Abigail's dog! That's just the way her mother described him."

She remembered that the dog's name was Noodles. She waited until the bushy-faced terrier came closer, and then she called him by name. Instantly the dog began to whine. He reared up on his hind legs, and she petted him. "It's all right, Noodles. You're going to be back home soon."

Juliet was almost to the house when the old man that she had seen before came out onto the porch. He was wearing worn brown trousers and a gray coat over a faded checkered shirt. He had an old soft hat shoved back on his head.

"Hello, there," he said quietly. "Who might

you be?" He was not a big man, and there was nothing in his manner to frighten Juliet. He had mild brown eyes. White hair poked out from under his hat, and he smiled. "And what are you doing way out here?"

"It's kind of a long story," Juliet said.

"Well, if it's going to be very long, maybe you and I had better have something to drink. Do you like hot tea?"

"Oh, yes sir! I like it a lot. My mother makes it for us. She gets it all the way from England."

"Why, so do I. And I was about to make myself a cup. I've got some water boiling right now. Why don't you sit on the porch here? I've got two rocking chairs. You take this one."

Juliet was glad he didn't ask her in. She knew that would not please her parents. The man was a stranger. In fact, she suddenly was pretty sure her parents wouldn't like her being here at all.

However, she sat down on the rocking chair. The dogs crowded up until she was completely surrounded. There were all kinds. And all seemed friendly—as if they were pets. She especially paid attention to Abigail's dog.

"I found you, Noodles," she said, "and I'll bet I have you home soon."

In a short time, the old man came back out onto the porch. He carried a brown tray. There were two cups and a teakettle on it. There

97

were also sugar and cream. He put down the tray on a low wooden table and poured Juliet some tea. "You can have sugar and cream if you like."

"Yes. I do like it." Juliet put the sugar and cream in her tea. After tasting it, she said, "Oh, this is good!"

"I like mine with sugar and cream, too."

"My name is Juliet Jones."

"I'm very happy to meet you, Miss Juliet Jones. My name is Liles."

"I met a friend of yours," Juliet said. "Mr. Sands. He told me he knew you back when you were boys in school together."

"Oh yes. That was a long time ago," Mr. Liles said. "We were good friends once."

Juliet began petting the dogs that acted the most interested in her. "Do you like living out here by yourself, Mr. Liles?"

"For the most part I do. I lost my wife some time ago, and I just didn't like staying in the town where we had lived. Since I grew up around here, I thought I'd come back and see if I'd like living here again."

"I bet you'd like it better if people came to see you. And if you went to town to see people. Mr. Sands said he asked you to come and visit him, but you never came."

"I guess after my wife died," Mr. Liles said, "I just didn't feel much like going out and talking to people. But I've made lots of friends lately. Here are all my friends." He waved his hand toward the dogs. Several of them saw what he did, and right away they came to him. A little one jumped into his lap, and he petted it. "I've always loved dogs," he said quietly.

"That's why you have so many of them?"

Mr. Liles pulled out a pipe. He stuffed it with tobacco and then lit it with a kitchen match. After he got it puffing, he looked at Juliet and slowly began to talk. But he didn't talk about the dogs. "My children live far away, one in California and one out in New York. I don't see them very much. I thought if I'd come back here where I grew up, I might find a little peace."

"It seems awfully lonesome out here in the woods."

"I suppose it is. I do get lonesome," he admitted. He sipped some tea. Then he puffed on his pipe for a while. There was sadness in his eyes. "I always meant to get to know people better. But living way out here, it's just not easy."

"I saw you in town once or twice."

"Oh yes. I go to town when I need supplies. But somehow I just never talk to anyone. Don't ever have any company out here."

"Do you ever go to church?"

"I did." Mr. Liles nodded. "When I was a boy. The white church down on the corner of Elm Street."

"Why, that's my church!"

"Is it, now? Well, it was a fine church then, and I suppose it still is."

"I like it! We'd be glad to have you come to visit us, Mr. Liles."

"Well, I don't have very nice clothes to wear to church, Juliet Jones."

"Oh, that wouldn't matter at our church," Juliet said quickly.

She wanted to ask him again about the dogs. But she could not think of a good way to do it. Finally she just said, "You have a lot of dogs."

"Oh yes. I've always enjoyed dogs. This one was first. He just came to me one day." He reached down and put his hand on the head of the small, scruffy brown dog. "His name is Bo."

"Hello, Bo," Juliet said.

Bo barked.

"He likes most people," Mr. Liles said. "He goes out wandering a lot." He hesitated for a moment, then petted Bo again. "When he came back home one day, he had this fellow with him." He touched a reddish dog with short wiry hair. "He didn't seem to have a home, so I started feeding him. And he just stayed. Been here ever since."

"Is that the way all these dogs got here?"

"Pretty much. They just took up with Bo and me. I don't know who they used to belong to. Some of them acted real hungry when they came, and it gives me pleasure to feed them. Dogs need love, too. Like I said, I just let them stay."

Juliet sipped at her tea, thinking hard. She knew that she had to say something about the missing dogs. "Mr. Liles, did you know that there are some dogs in town that have been reported stolen?"

"Why, no. I didn't know that."

"Well, it's true. A lot of dogs have just disappeared. And the police are looking into it."

"I never read the newspaper. I suppose there was a story about it."

"Maybe. I don't know if there was," Juliet said. Then she went on, carefully. "I can tell you're just a nice man who likes dogs. But yesterday I met a little girl who had lost her dog. Her name was Abigail. And I'm sure this is her dog right here. His name is Noodles."

When she spoke his name, the dog perked up his ears. Then he barked.

"Oh, I'm awfully sorry to hear that! That one just followed Bo home the other day. He didn't have a collar or anything, and I was afraid he'd starve to death out here in these woods. We'll have to take him back at once. Can you show me where she lives?"

"Yes, I will." Juliet frowned then. "And one more thing, Mr. Liles, that I think you ought to do . . ."

"What's that, Miss Juliet?"

"Maybe you ought to go by the police station and talk to Chief Bender. And tell him about these dogs out here. He might want to put something in the paper about them—for the people who have lost their dogs."

"I guess that would be a good idea. But if that little girl is really sad, we ought to take her dog back right away . . ."

"It's getting late," Juliet said. "And you'd have to come back in the dark. I can take Noodles back to Abigail by myself. Maybe we could just meet tomorrow? You can come in and meet me at the police station. I know Chief Bender. He won't be mad. He'll just be glad to find out where the dogs are."

"All right. I'll do that. Nine o'clock. Let me get you a leash to put on this fellow here."

Mr. Liles found an old leather leash.

Juliet slipped it around Noodles's neck. "Come along, boy," she said. As they left the yard, she turned around and said, "I'll see you tomorrow at nine o'clock, Mr. Liles."

"I'll be there." Then the old man said, "You're my first visitor, Juliet. I enjoyed your visit."

"I did, too. And I'll come back, if you'll let me. And then maybe you can come and visit *my* house."

"That'll be something to look forward to."

He looked around at the many dogs. "I suppose I'll be losing some of these. But if their owners are looking for them, it's right that they have them back."

Juliet felt a little guilty. She was making Mr. Liles sad. But she knew that telling him had been the right thing to do. "Good-bye. I'll see you tomorrow," she said. And then she and Noodles left.

One of the happiest times in Juliet's life was when she walked up to the door of the Harrington family and knocked.

The door opened, and there stood Abigail. She saw her dog and cried his name. "Noodles—Noodles, you're home!"

Juliet had never felt more pleased. Both of Abigail's parents thanked her over and over, and she felt warm and happy inside. She had solved a mystery, and things had turned out very well.

By the time Juliet got home, her parents were getting a little worried. She told her story, and they listened.

Then her dad said, "Well, we're glad you found the dog. But, Juliet, you must never, never, never go to a stranger's house all by yourself. You did a very foolish thing."

"But he's such a nice man, and he's so lonesome!"

"We know that, Juliet. But some strangers aren't nice. And you can't tell just by looking at them. Next time, come and ask first. All right?" Juliet's mother said.

"All right, Mom. I will. I'm sorry I didn't use my head. But I'd prayed about it . . . and I really thought I needed to find Abigail's dog, and . . ."

"Just be careful in the future. The Lord doesn't tell us to do things that are foolish. Remember, not everyone is nice like Mr. Liles."

"I know now, Dad," Juliet said. "I promise."

When she went up to bed, Joe came in to say, "I wish I'd been with you."

"He's a nice man, Joe. We've got to go back and be friends to him. He's very lonesome."

"Suits me. Maybe he knows some leaves and trees that I don't know. And we can take him some of Mom's cookies and eat some ourselves."

Juliet laughed at him. "All right. We'll do that," she said.

12

A Happy Ending

Juliet Jones was happy. As always, she awoke suddenly and—still lying in bed—began singing a Bible verse she liked very much:

"This is the day, this is the day
    That the Lord hath made, that the Lord
        hath made.
    I will rejoice,
    I will rejoice,
    And be glad in it . . ."

She sang the song softly two or three times. She wished again that she could sing as well as Jenny White.

But finally she got out of bed and went through her morning routine. It did not take her long to wash her face and brush her hair and get dressed. By that time, she was hearing somebody moving around downstairs. Juliet started singing again, this time much louder, "This is the day that the Lord hath made . . ."

Her brother's room was at the top of the stairs. Juliet managed to bump into him as he came stumbling out his door. As always, he was sleepy-eyed and could barely see where he was going.

"Why do you have to go around singing at the top of your voice so early in the morning?" he complained.

"Don't be such a growly bear, Joe!" Juliet reached over and ruffled his red hair. "'Red-headed peckerwood sittin' on a fence, trying to make a dollar out of fifteen cents,'" she teased.

Teasing always infuriated Joe. "It's not right to go around singing so early in the morning!" he shouted. "I'm gonna wait until tonight when *you're* sleepy. And I'm going to start singing about Too Smart Jones. 'Here lie the bones of Too Smart Jones!'"

They argued for a while. Then Juliet said, "Oh, come on. Let's go eat breakfast."

They ran down the stairs and into the dining room. Just as they got there, their father came in from the kitchen. He was carrying a big platter covered with a lid. "Good morning," he said. "I decided to make breakfast this morning and give your mother a break."

"Oh no!" Joe moaned. He slapped his hands over his eyes. "Not again!"

"And what's that supposed to mean?" Mr. Jones asked loudly.

"Nothing," Joe mumbled. He plunked down in his chair.

Juliet took the chair across from him. "I think it's nice that you help Mom do some of her work, Dad," she said.

"Well, I'm glad I get a little respect around here!"

Everyone in the house except Mr. Jones himself dreaded the days when Father decided to help Mother cook. Mr. Jones could build a bridge or a skyscraper, but he had a hard time in the kitchen. However, he insisted on "helping" Mrs. Jones from time to time.

Then their mother came in. She said brightly, "Well, children, isn't this nice? Your father has decided to help me cook again."

"I think it's wonderful, Mom," Juliet said at once.

"Thank you, Juliet," her father said. "Now, let me get the rest of our breakfast, and then we'll have the blessing, and then we can eat."

As soon as he went back into the kitchen, Joe moaned and said, "We're all going to die!"

"Oh, don't be foolish! Your father does very well."

Actually the meal was not too bad today. The eggs were fried a little too hard. And the toast was burned, but it had been carefully scraped. The sausages were black on the outside. But everyone in the family managed to eat breakfast.

Mrs. Jones smiled at her husband more than once. "Not many husbands would help their wives cook unless she were sick. I appreciate it."

Mr. Jones looked very pleased. "I'm glad to do it. I never did feel comfortable around these men who think housework is sissy. I don't see anything sissy about it."

Juliet looked at her father. Of all the men in the world, Dad was not a sissy. He lifted weights, and ran, and swam laps, and worked out under the sun so that he was tanned and healthy all the time.

"I hope you'll help *your* wife, if you ever get one, Joe."

"Sure, Dad. I'll do that," Joe said.

As Mr. Jones got ready to eat a huge forkful of eggs, he asked, "What about Mr. Liles, Juliet?"

"Well, it's like I told you last night. He's going to the police station today at nine o'clock. He'll explain to Chief Bender what happened. I told him I'd go along and explain, too."

"I hope he doesn't put Mr. Liles in jail," Joe said.

"Oh, he won't do that!" their mother said quickly. "After all, he didn't *steal* the dogs."

"Well, he didn't report them either," Joe said darkly. "You never know. The FBI might get after him. Or the CIA."

Mr. Jones grinned broadly. His teeth shone white against his tanned face. "I think you're the one, instead of Juliet, who's getting too caught up in mysteries."

Juliet finished her breakfast. "I'm going on down to the station now. If it's all right. Or do you want me to help you with the dishes, Dad?"

"No. You go ahead."

Joe hopped up from the table. "I'll go, too."

The two of them ran most of the way to the police station.

The first person Juliet saw there was Mr. Liles himself. He was standing by the station door. It looked as if he had just arrived.

He had brought the brown dog with him, and Bo ran to meet Juliet. He kept jumping up as she petted him.

"Well, here I am," Mr. Liles said. "I hope we can get this thing straightened out."

Juliet thought the old man looked a little worried.

"Don't worry, Mr. Liles. We've been praying about all this, and it's going to be all right. You'll like Chief Bender. He's a nice man."

The three of them went inside. There they found the chief, sitting at his desk reading a *Popular Mechanics* magazine. He put it down on the desk and grinned. "I'm attending to my official duties," he said. "Reading about the latest cars people can steal. What are you kids doing here?"

"Chief Bender, this is Mr. Liles. He lives over sort of north of town. Out in the woods past the transformer station."

"Why, sure. I've seen you around town a few times, haven't I?" The chief got up and came around the desk. He shook hands with Mr. Liles. The chief towered over the old man. He had been a wrestler when he was younger. He was still large and strong.

Mr. Liles looked around nervously. "Well, I guess I've come in to confess, Chief."

Chief Bender grew serious. "Confess to what, Mr. Liles?"

"Well—"

"Let me tell it, Mr. Liles," Juliet said quickly. She explained to Chief Bender how Mr. Liles had allowed stray dogs to stay at his house. She was also careful to say that he did not know that any of them belonged to anyone.

"Doesn't seem that's a very serious crime," the chief said. "There have been some dogs reported missing. But from what I understand, a lot of people just didn't care about their dogs anyway. Just let them run loose."

"I already took one back." Juliet told how she had returned Abigail's dog. "She was so glad to get it back. Her parents were, too."

"Well, there may be one or two more that the owners would like to have back. Tell you what, Mr. Liles," he said. "Why don't you keep the dogs a while longer? I'll just run a little story in the newspaper. We'll say that some dogs have been found. And if the owners come to the police station, we'll put them in touch with the man who may have the dog they're looking for. I won't mention your name, of course. Perhaps you'd better leave a description of all the dogs."

"I'll be glad to do that," Mr. Liles said. "I really didn't mean any harm, Chief. Most of them seemed half starved. So it just never occurred to me that they might belong to somebody."

Mr. Liles sat down. He began to tell what each dog looked like. Juliet wrote down all the information neatly. Then she handed the list to Chief Bender.

"This ought to do it," the chief said. "By the way, I think you knew my dad, Mr. Liles. His name was Charlie."

"Charlie Bender! You're Charlie Bender's boy? Why, we were boyhood friends."

"Yeah, he's been gone for about ten years now. But he mentioned you many times. He said you two fished together sometimes down at Pike River."

"That we did. Those were the good days. I think of them often. And I think of your father. He was a good man, Chief."

"I still fish in the river myself. Why don't you go with me some Saturday?"

"Why, that would be nice."

"Good. I've got a boat and all the equipment. Let's say next Saturday I pick you up about dawn. We'll get us some beauties."

"I'd like that very much."

As they left the police station and walked toward the Jones house, Juliet said, "See. You've got another friend. Chief Bender. Now you'll have somebody to fish with."

"That will be good. I see now that I've been keeping to myself too much."

When they got to her house, Juliet introduced Mr. Liles to her parents. Both of them welcomed him in. Besides that, they insisted that he come back for dinner next Monday night.

"Now, tomorrow's Sunday," Mr. Jones said. "We'd be glad to have you come to visit our church."

"And it's his church, too!" Juliet said quickly. She turned to Mr. Liles. "He told me he went to our church when he was a boy."

"It's a different building today," Mr. Liles said. "The one I went to was pretty old even then. But it's in the same place."

"Why, there might be some of our church members that would remember you, Mr. Liles," Mrs. Jones said. "We have some people who have belonged to the church for years and years."

"I want you to come, Mr. Liles," Juliet said. "Really I do."

"All right. I guess I will."

"And I'll show you some of my inventions right now!" Joe told him. "Come upstairs."

As soon as the two left the room, Mr. Jones turned to Juliet. "I think your mystery solving turned out well this time, Juliet. In fact, I think you've given a new life to a man who needed it."

They were still talking about Mr. Liles, when suddenly a loud crash sounded from upstairs.

Everybody jumped.

"What in the world was that?" Juliet asked.

The three of them started for the stairs. When they got to the bottom of the steps, though, they met Joe rushing down.

"Hey, don't get uptight," he said. "Just wanted to let you know one of my inventions went a little bit wrong."

"You're not hurt, are you?"

"Oh no. Everything's fine. Mr. Liles is OK, too."

Then Mr. Liles appeared at the top of the stairs. He was smiling. "I suppose Thomas Edison had a few of his inventions go wrong, too. Maybe I can help you fix it, Joe."

"OK, Mr. Liles."

Joe dashed back upstairs and disappeared with his new friend.

Mrs. Jones put her arms around Juliet. She whispered, "Sherlock Holmes the Second, you did very well this time."

Juliet Jones was happy. She hugged her mother and her father. Then she ran out into the front yard, followed by the scruffy brown dog. She was singing, "This is the day, this is the day that the Lord hath made. I will rejoice and be glad in it . . ."

Then she stopped and picked up Bo. "Bo, this is a good day for girl detectives. And it's a good day for scruffy brown dogs too." She kissed him on the nose.

Bo wiggled to be put down. Then the two of them ran around and around the yard, Bo barking and Juliet singing her song. Finally she leaned over and patted Bo on the head one more time. "The mystery is solved, Bo. Now you and I will be seeing a lot of each other!"

Get swept away in the many Gilbert Morris Adventures from Moody Press:

"Too Smart" Jones Series

Join Juliet "Too Smart" Jones and her homeschooled friends as they attempt to solve exciting mysteries. Active Series for ages 7-12.

Dixie Morris Animal Adventures

Follow the exciting adventures of this animal lover as she learns more of God and His character through her many adventures underneath the Big Top. Ten Book Series for ages 7-12.

The Daystar Voyages

Join the crew of the Daystar as they traverse the wide expanse of space. Adventure and danger abound, but they learn time and again that God is truly the Master of the Universe. Active Series for ages 10-14.

Bonnets and Bugles Series

Follow good friends Leah Carter and Jeff Majors as they experience danger, intrigue, compassion, and love in these civil war adventures. Ten Book Series for ages 10-14.

The Seven Sleepers Series

Go with Josh and his friends as they are sent by Goél, their spiritual leader, on dangerous and challenging voyages to conquer the forces of darkness in the new world. Ten Book Series for ages 10-14. Watch for the new Lost Chronicles of the Seven Sleepers!